Stories by Contemporary Writers from Shanghai

WHEN
A BABY
IS BORN...

This book is edited and designed by the Editorial Committee of
Cultural China series

Managing Directors: Wang Youbu, Xu Naiqing
Editorial Director: Wu Ying
Series Editor: Wang Jiren
Editors: Daniel Clutton, Ye Jiasheng

Text by Cheng Naishan
Translation by Benjamin Chang

Interior and Cover Design: Wang Wei
Cover Image: Getty Images

ISBN: 978-1-60220-215-3

Address any comments about *When a Baby Is Born ...* to:

Better Link Press
99 Park Ave
New York, NY 10016
USA
or
Shanghai Press and Publishing Development Company
F 7 Donghu Road, Shanghai, China (200031)
Email: comments_betterlinkpress@hotmail.com

Printed in China by Shanghai Donnelley Printing Co. Ltd.

1 2 3 4 5 6 7 8 9 10

WHEN A BABY IS BORN...

By Cheng Naishan

Better Link Press

Preface

English readers will be presented with a set of 12 pocket books. These books contain outstanding novellas written by 12 writers from Shanghai over the past 30 years. Most of the writers were born in Shanghai from the late 1940's to the late 1950's. They started their literary careers during or after the 1980's. For various reasons, most of them lived and worked in the lowest social strata in other cities or in rural areas for much of their adult lives. As a result they saw much of the world and learned lessons from real life before finally returning to Shanghai. They embarked on their literary careers for various reasons, but most of them were simply passionate about writing. The writers are involved in a variety of occupations, including university professors, literary editors, leaders of literary institutions and professional writers. The diversity of topics covered in these novellas will lead readers to discover the different experiences and motivations of the authors. Readers will encounter a fascinating range of esthetic convictions as they analyze the authors' distinctive artistic skills and writing styles. Generally speaking, a realistic writing style dominates most of their literary works. The literary works they have elaborately created are a true reflection of drastic social changes, as well as differing perspectives towards urban life in Shanghai. Some works created by avant-garde writers have been selected in order to present a variety of styles. No matter what writing styles they adopt though, these writers have enjoyed a definite place, and exerted a positive influence, in Chinese literary circles over the past three decades.

Known as the "Paris of the Orient" around the world, Shanghai was already an international metropolis in the 1920's and 1930's. During that period, Shanghai was China's economic, cultural and literary center. A high number of famous Chinese writers lived, created and published their literary works in Shanghai, including, Lu Xun, Guo Moruo, Mao Dun and Ba Jin. Today, Shanghai has become a globalized metropolis. Writers who have pursued a literary career in the past 30 years are now faced with new challenges and opportunities. I am confident that some of them will produce other fine and influential literary works in the future. I want to make it clear that this set of pocket books does not include all representative Shanghai writers. When the time is ripe, we will introduce more representative writers to readers in the English-speaking world.

Wang Jiren
Series Editor

Chapter 1

He always had bad luck. For all his efforts, he only managed to get a middle bunk in the sleeper car. Also, as the train didn't depart at the local terminal the luggage racks were already jammed full by the time he got on. He didn't appear too worried however, thinking that his ticket entitled him to a space. He was already accustomed to handling a situation like this. All he needed to do was to give the luggage a sidewise push and squeeze his own in with a hard shove. Spitting out the cigarette butt forcefully, Tang Dawei surveyed the luggage rack with a determined look to see if he could find a space. Although the universe is infinitely vast and the space that a human being needs is so tiny in comparison, a person sometimes has to struggle for that tiny space for all his life.

There on the rack lay a gleaming beautiful red and black rolling tote bag designed in the latest style, taking up the space of two or three suitcases. What right did it have to behave with such arrogance? Was it because of its "fancy" style? He took the liberty of adjusting the rolling tote bag to make space for his old faded traveling bag. A slogan popular in the Cultural Revolution was still discernible on it. The bag was anything but suitable for traveling.

"Hey, what's going on, man?" A man wearing a T-shirt came over, staring at him in a menacing way. It was the owner of the fancy rolling tote bag.

"Nothing. I'm trying to make space for my luggage." Unperturbed, Tang Dawei squeezed his traveling bag in and carefully adjusted it. In the bag were two pounds of bright red woolen yarns for his wife. They felt fluffy and soft even through the lining of the bag. What a great feeling! With delight and uncertainty, he touched the bag again. He experienced a sensation he had last had when touching his infant son's fleshy body in a swaddle years ago. This was the first time since the day of their marriage that he'd bought his wife an expensive gift. It cost as much as thirty-six yuan! It was Xiao'an (Little An) who had made the selection for him at the hotel gift store. He thought the color was too loud and couldn't make up his mind. She scoffed at him for being conservative. "Too loud? No way. Don't you know the seventy-or-eighty-year-old foreign ladies are dressed in bright red?" She had talked Dawei into making the purchase, which was not entirely to her credit; he himself preferred bright red, synonymous with happiness and joy. His wife never gave a thought to herself but always made a point of reserving the best for her husband and son. If he hadn't chosen a feminine color, the woolen yarns would have ended up with someone other than herself, as was usually the case. He knew that his wife would be happy when she saw the gift and tried to picture her delight in his mind's eye, but he drew a blank. For as long as he had known her, she was capable of no more than a faint smile when she was happy. Even when he had received his letter of admission to college, her smile was wistful. The toughness of her life had knocked all laughter out of the poor woman. He was determined to delight her this time.

Feeling upset at his brand new rolling tote bag being pushed aside, the man in the T-shirt readjusted its position and muttered to himself in Shanghai dialect, "Stupid ass! Nothing short of a dumb country bumpkin!"

So, the man was from Shanghai. Little wonder he was so cocky and arrogant. By the mere possession of their Shanghai residence cards, the Shanghainese were in the habit of presenting themselves as the lords of the earth in their dealings with outsiders. Dawei refused to budge and being furious he grabbed the man in the T-shirt by the collar and said, "Shut your foul mouth! I dare you to say that again!"

"Say what again? What did I ... say?" the Shanghainese stammered, his face ashen white, while lifting his hand to fend off a possible blow. What a coward! The man's weakness added fuel to his fury. Dawei would have gladly let go of him if he had been man enough to initiate a few punches.

"Watch your language or I'll beat you up!" Dawei responded in the same dialect. The man in the T-shirt was stunned, little expecting that the big guy who was coarsely dressed and wearing only a pair of sandals would be a native of Shanghai. At this moment, a pregnant woman came up, to make peace apparently. She appeared to be the wife of the man in the T-shirt. To pacify

Dawei, she said in her soft Shanghai dialect, "I'm very sorry, sir. We're all from the same city, let's be friends ..."

"Forget it! When the journey is over, we'll each go our own way. So why bother?"

"Come, come, why don't we calm down and keep quiet?"

The passengers tried to intervene to mediate the dispute. However, Dawei was still furious. He hated the superiority complex characteristic of Shanghai residents, who tended to mock and discriminate against the non-natives of Shanghai. They were a disgrace to the city and he hated their guts. Today he had experienced their snobbishness at first hand and had been unable to swallow the insult. He felt the blood pumping fast through his veins. Just then, he felt a gentle tap on his shoulder and turned around to see the frightened eyes of Xiao'an, who had come to see him off. The poor girl was scared by all the hostility. Only then did Dawei release his grip of the collar of Mr. T-shirt. Bad timing! It was too bad that she should have witnessed his savage behavior.

"Now you've seen the other side of me." He scratched his head, feeling awkward.

"Take it easy," she said, giving him a conciliatory smile. "Don't lose your temper. It's not worth fighting over the luggage rack."

Of course, he should let such a trivial incident pass, but he was bitter that life was unfair and unjust. Those who have are given even more, while those who are poor lose the little that they have. He cast an angry look at the gleaming rolling tote bag ... Anyway, let's not get into that.

"What a stroke of luck you had getting a middle berth!" she crept up to his berth and said. "It saves you the trouble of climbing up and down too far and you've got the air-conditioning. You see, you're lucky."

She was an optimist. If a bottle was half full, instead of complaining about the half-filled bottle, she would say, "Good! Half a bottle is better than nothing." That was the right attitude to have towards life. Look at Xiao'an, who was engaged in an animated chat with Mr. T-shirt in their common dialect, as if they had been buddies for years. She was the last person to get into an argument, being the kind of girl you just couldn't help loving at first sight. His berth being right across from Mr. T-shirt's, Dawei could hardly imagine crossing narrow paths with his deadly foe again in such a manner. But it looked as if Mr. T-shirt had been smoothed over by the sweet smile of Xiao'an and he even tried to push his fancy rolling tote bag further aside as a gesture of good will, even though it stayed put. Women seem to have a flair for handling conflict situations better than men. No wonder "lady diplomacy" is much encouraged and practiced in foreign countries.

"Coming from the same city, you two should help each other during the trip," said Xiao'an. "Besides, this lady happens to be pregnant. That's all the more reason to show some concern for one another. You have a 36-hour trip ahead of you."

Her words left him feeling ashamed. Actually, he should have been the one doing the admonishing, not the girl who had been under his wing over the past twenty days. She had returned to her own way of doing things, which she considered safe now. Not only had she walked out from under his wing, but she'd also gone a step further by trying to protect him. Wasn't that embarrassing to him as a man?

"I told you not to come and see me off in this heat. I'm not pleased that you've ignored me." He was being grumpy and trying to reclaim some of his masculine dignity. But in his heart he was appreciative of her thoughtfulness and felt good about it. "You know, I left home when I was only seventeen. Since then I have been traveling a lot on my own and I am used to it ..." he babbled on and on about things she wasn't interested in.

"I came because I am leaving in the

afternoon and I've got plenty of time," she said, trying to justify herself. He felt sorry to make her look bad.

In just a few minutes, they would each go their own way. She was disappointed with his nonchalant talk in the precious last moments before the train departed. Finally, he came to the point.

"You're marvellous, Xiao'an. Say hello to your boyfriend for me."

"Sure. I'll have him write to you." Her face was beaming with smiles. "I'm sure you'll like him."

"You've passed the age when you needed to consult your mother on every matter. You can handle things by yourself. Listen, whatever you do, follow your inclination. Even if something goes wrong later on, you'll have no regrets. You're actually on the right track. You're a courageous girl." He wished she would stay as cheerful and optimistic as ever.

"Thank you for your kindness," she replied excitedly.

The conductor brusquely announced the departure of the train. Dawei held the door for her, fearing it would slam shut, and gave her his parting advice, "Keep going now that we are out of our cozy nests. There's no turning back, whatever happens. There's no future in looking back."

Her eyes full of tenderness, she looked up at him from the platform, expecting a few more parting words. He admired her as a girl of unusual qualities, for it was she who had challenged his conceptions of Shanghai residents, the seemingly pampered Shanghai girls in particular. He was suddenly seized with an urge to tell her that he was very fond of her. But the words remained unspoken as the train pulled out of the station. It is characteristic of human beings that the sincerest words are usually uttered last and that they feel compelled to release the feelings pulsing through their hearts and minds when they realize they are going to lose sight of the ones they love.

She jogged after the train, shouting to him as she went, but then slowed to a helpless halt. He saw her turn around, her head hanging low and her hands deep in her skirt pockets. She must have been weeping. Frailty, thy name is woman. Although she was a brilliant metallurgical engineer, dealing with alloy metal hard as a rock day in and day out, she was in essence a vulnerable girl. On the platform, her figure appeared so tiny, thin, and weak that her boyfriend once said lovingly that he would steal her away and keep her safe. But he had worried unnecessarily. Xiao'an would become strong, brave, and determined like a fresh flower endowed with great energy and vitality. Farewell, Xiao'an. May your life be full of blessings!

"Want some tea? This is authentic Shaoxing tea and it's not available in Northern China."

After Dawei returned to his berth, Mr. T-shirt offered his tea can to him as if nothing unpleasant had ever happened between them.

"Are you going to catch a connecting train in Beijing?" Mr. T-shirt asked.

"Yes. I work in a mining town in the Northwest, located in the Gobi Desert."

"Wow! It's quite far away!" Mr. T-shirt heaved a sigh.

"How about you? Do you work in Beijing?"

"No, we're going there on vacation. I was able to secure two weeks' sick leave and my wife started her maternity leave ahead of time. Here we are, ready for fun," he said in a cheerful and complacent tone.

"Two weeks' sick leave? That's really neat!"

"Not a big deal. My doctor and I are on good terms with each other. I work in a department store on Huaihai Road, and we sort of ... you know what I mean?" Mr. T-shirt missed Dawei's sarcastic note and went on trumpeting his own smartness.

"Late autumn is the best season for sightseeing in Beijing."

Out of courtesy, Dawei kept the conversation going, but in reality he loathed talking to strangers on the train.

"First we'll go to the beach and then tour the city of Beijing," Mr. T-shirt yawned. "I've visited many cities, but none of them are anything as clean and orderly as Shanghai. My wife's due date is drawing near and I want to take her on a trip which will do some good for our future child. This is what we call 'early education,' as early as the fetus in the womb. We want to nurture our child in the best possible environment. Since we're only going to have one kid, a little investment makes sense."

It seemed to Dawei that Mr. T-shirt was one of the privileged, concerning himself with travel, education, nurturing his child, etc., etc. These things were only possible when food and clothing were no longer a concern. There was no lack of such fortunate people in the metropolis of Shanghai. Dawei was green with envy, but convinced that he would have been in their ranks if he still retained his Shanghai residence card.

"How come you've set up home in such a remote area? My God, the Gobi Desert!" Mr. T-shirt took a sip of tea. "You were sent there as a 'cultured youth' to do farming in the country-side or work in the factory? You were an easy target I guess. I finished middle school in 1968 when all the graduates were shipped to the countryside. But I stuck it out, even when I was harassed with drums and gongs and slogans ev-ery day. I guarded my residence card as my lifeline. I'd rather be a night soil collector in Shanghai than a high offi-cial in another city." As he said this, he pounded on the table to show his deter-mination.

"Later on, I was assigned a job in a

neighborhood factory and before long transferred to a department store on Huaihai Road as a shop assistant. People flocked to ask me for help getting hold of scarce goods. The job brought me a lot of fringe benefits I hadn't dared to dream of before." He reclined in his seat with an air of self-complacency, intoxicated with his glorious past.

"Well," Mr. T-shirt seemed to hit upon an idea, "why don't you apply for admission to college? It's a good way around the problem of getting permanent residence in Shanghai. A lot of my former classmates did it."

"But I'm already a college grad. When I graduated I was sent back to work in the mining enterprise I'd come from."

"Which means," Mr. T-shirt stamped his feet, "that you may be married. In that case it would be almost impossible for you to transfer back to Shanghai now." He showed pity and sympathy, as the average Shanghainese usually did to former fellow residents that strayed to other parts of the country, unless they went to Hong Kong and Macao. If there was one thing Dawei couldn't stand, it was being patronized. However, with Xiao'an's tolerant smile still fresh in his mind, he was not in the mood for another argument.

Dawei wasn't positive whether he belonged to the category of "cultured youth" or not. He had volunteered to go to the Northwestern region long before the words "cultured youth" were coined. That was way back in 1962 when he made his own decision and registered as a volunteer for work in the interior of the country. He still hadn't graduated from senior high school, but he wanted to escape the oppressive family that brought him no happiness and never understood him ... But, it didn't make any sense bringing all that up again. He had crossed the Rubicon. Whether he could be classified as a "cultured youth" was irrelevant to him, for he had neither a job to go to in Shanghai nor any friendly government policy to open doors for him. In 1977 he was admitted to Northwestern Industrial University and was top of his class, in age at least. After graduation, he went back to his former job and was promoted from a regular welder to a technician and before long to a metallurgical engineer. His childhood dream had come true. Even as a kid he had aspired to become an engineer, influenced by a huge billboard showing a confident-looking, bespectacled civil engineer who was holding a triangular ruler. Against the stereotyped image of the engineer, Dawei found his own appearance laughable—a brawny six-footer, dark-skinned, robust, and dull. He was nicknamed "Slow Camel." His hands were so big that the pen was buried in his palm whenever he wrote something. He wasn't the only exception to the stereotype. None of the other engineers who attended the Ministry-sponsored metallurgical conference looked like the one on the signboard. There was no telling that Xiao'an was also an engineer, and with a red scarf around her neck, she could have passed for a student. Each individual's image was shaped by his or her life experience. And in reality each individual was more lively and vivid than the lifeless figure under the painter's brush. Life had never been easy for him but he had made it his way. The secret was that rather than placing himself at the mercy of Providence, he took destiny in his own hands.

"Do you often come back to Shanghai for a visit?" Mr. T-shirt asked. Dawei gave a wry smile, reluctant to talk to the small-minded guy.

He rarely visited Shanghai. In fact, he had been there once in the past twenty years, and he had been forgotten by his home city. His parents had passed away, and his stepmother along with his half brother and sister treated him like a stranger. He no longer considered his roots as being beside the Huangpu River, but in the newly emerging mining town in the Gobi Desert which was home to his wife and son. He was sure they were sitting by the lamp, counting down the hours of his trip, and waiting eagerly for his return.

"What does your father do? Does he have any connections?" Mr. T-shirt was bent on getting to the bottom of things. He acted more like an inexperienced preacher seizing every moment to convince his audience of the unquestionable superiority of Shanghai.

Dawei gave a big yawn. If he really felt inclined to answer the question, he could astound the man with the standing and wealth his family had once had! His grandfather had owned a medium-sized factory that employed about three hundred workers. After the factory was nationalized, the quarterly dividend that was drawn from it amounted to as much as three thousand yuan! Being a titular director of the factory, his father didn't get involved in routine management, but took a long leave of absence to indulge in his passion for bridge. In December 1966, he gassed himself in the family oven, unable to bear the fanatic mobsters' humiliation and physical abuse after a life of comfort and luxury ... Dawei, of course, had no intention of discussing his private life with this buffoon who he met by chance.

Mr. T-shirt wouldn't give up and took out a pack of cards. "Let me tell your fortune and see if you will transfer back to Shanghai." So saying, he flipped out a card and said mysteriously, "You see, it's the Queen of Hearts, which means you need a woman's help. Is that your wife, I mean the lady I saw just now? She's quite young ..."

What was he talking about? Some people had no common sense. When they saw a woman was in the company of a man, they jumped to the conclu-

sion that they were either legitimate
spouses or illegitimate lovers. Dawei
didn't bother correcting him, and ex-
cusing himself, he retired to his bunk
to avoid further harassment from this
over-zealous busybody. The sweet, love-
ly figure again rose in his mind's eye.
He no longer worried about the girl
who had seemed so vulnerable the first
time they met. Behind the frail appearance and meek smile was a strong willed
woman who stuck to her principles with
absolute conviction. She was about to
embark with courage and confidence on
the path to a true and full life.

If God existed, she would be his
favorite creature, and if seeds of happiness existed, she would be a lucky
seed kissed and nurtured by breeze
and sunlight.

Twenty days ago, he ran into her on a train to a summer beach resort where he was going to a conference. She looked innocent and uncertain. Carrying a bulky bag on her back, she was trying to squeeze through the narrow cramped passageway, only to be frowned upon by the conductor and fellow passengers. She looked bewildered and pathetic. She was talking anxiously to the conductor, seemingly to get some information; but she was ignored, her strong Shanghai accent seemingly acting as a barrier to communication. The scene somehow aroused a sympathy in him for a fellow native of Shanghai, although he was usually unmoved by such a situation. Seeing the heavy bulky bag on her back and beads of perspiration on her face, he was ready to give his seat to her. Twenty years of tough living had desensitized him to what he considered the dated etiquette of "ladies first," although he had come from a family where such a code of behavior was emphasized and instilled in his mind. In his eyes, there was little difference between male and female. Didn't his wife work like a man? A female was as good as a male. But the scene on the train prompted him to lend a helping hand to the timid, delicate Shanghai girl. He decided to give her his seat the moment she managed to wedge her way through and reach him.

Instead of making it to his seat, she stopped at the row before him and leaned on the back of a seat, exhausted. A middle-aged man was sitting there, dangling his leg and engrossed in a graphic novel. Noticing the girl at his side, he moved across to the very edge of the seat, making sure there was no room left for the girl. What an asshole! Dawei immediately got to his feet, offering his seat to the girl, while the other passengers regarded him with quizzical looks as if to say, "Hey, what a lady's man." They were mostly petty merchants and small vendors plying their goods between the small stations on the short branch line, with the exception of some passengers heading for Star Sea Beach.

Without even thanking him, she took the seat. Dawei was sure her rudeness was not from being tired. She simply seemed accustomed to being taken care of and protected in life.

"Excuse me, but can you tell me whether I should get off at Luo Village for Star Sea Beach?" she asked timidly, embarrassed to disturb him.

"Yes."

"How many more stations are there

to go?"

He was amused by her question.
She wasn't taking a bus or a street car
and there was no need to worry about
missing a stop. To put her mind at ease,
he said, "It's another three hours yet."

"How do I get to River West Hotel? Is
it far from the railway station? Do you
know?"

How come she was going to the same
hotel? He noticed a wrinkled pink slip
in her hand, which turned out to be a
leaflet with detailed directions to the
site of the conference sponsored by the
Ministry of Metallurgical Engineering.
Was she a participant at the conference?
Was she a winner of the technological
design award? In any case he found
it difficult to associate the girl with
something like alloy metal. She might
be some old guy's young daughter who

had taken advantage of the conference to get a free vacation.

The conference leaflet was wrinkled beyond recognition. Look at her girlish face. She should have been at home, instead of traveling on her own and putting herself at the mercy of con men or worse.

He tried to force himself to take his eyes off her, but it was no use. She was a typical Shanghai girl. For twenty years since settling down in the Northwestern region, he hadn't mixed with any Shanghai girls, who he didn't think he had any chemistry with anymore. He still thought that Shanghai girls were the cutest in the country, but that was probably just due to favoritism on his part.

The girl was casually dressed, wearing a light blue cotton sweater and a dark blue denim skirt, plus white socks and tennis shoes with a blue lining. The outfit was well appropriate for rough travel, pretty and practical. Shanghai girls are usually at their best in making themselves presentable; as the saying goes, "The best food is in Guangdong and the latest fashion in Shanghai." It had never occurred to him that clothes, aside from their functional use in shielding the body and resisting the elements, had a decorative dimension like roses and musical notes. It pained him to think that his wife had passed the prime of her youth donned all day long in a shabby jacket modified from his discarded uniform. She had never had beautiful clothes to satisfy her feminine vanity. He admitted he was a loser lacking the cash needed to buy her colorful clothes. He imagined that with a well-built buxom body like his wife's would certainly look sharp in the girl's casual outfit. She was just as gutsy and tenacious as the main character in the Japanese movie *The Cry of the Distant Mountain*, who fought against all the odds to build a comfortable niche for her family, although her body was less shapely. His wife was far from being a fictional character, but she had been molded into a tough woman by the strenuous nature of her life.

The girl's timid eye scrutinized him silently. He wasn't sure whether *scrutinize* was the right word to use under the circumstances. Oddly, she had a special feature, or to be exact, a demeanor that kept him wondering whether he had met her before, which seemed unlikely since she could only have been a toddler at the time he lived in Shanghai.

"Are you from Shanghai?" For the first time in his life he had displayed a friendly, concerned gesture towards a stranger. "Why don't you follow me? I'm heading to the conference too." While saying this he went through the award-winning projects in his mind, trying to remember how many of them originated in Shanghai. He could only think of one, called "Boiler Dust Liquidating Device Model R." The project had called for a sophisticated design and couldn't have come from the hands of a girl who was clutching the traffic direction slip like a lucky charm.

"Thank you. You see how lucky I am!" She beamed. She was the kind of person who was liable to make a show of her gratitude. She felt that she had a lot to thank Providence for, having received Dawei's offer of help.

"Are you the only one representing Shanghai?" he asked, leading to more mocking stares from those who believed him to be either a womanizer or, worse, a swindler.

"Yes, just one from Shanghai. At first I hesitated to come, but I couldn't resist the temptation of a trip to the beach. It would be a shame to miss the chance, don't you think? Where are you from?"

"Gansu Province."

Rolling her eyes, she suddenly burst out, "So you're the one who came up with an innovative interpretation of electrolyte and got poisoned from chlorine in the lab. And your name is ...?"

Her loud voice caught the attention of the curious listeners around, which made him uncomfortable.

"Could I have your address just in case? I've been thinking about paying a visit out there."

There was no need for her to be in such a rush for his address as they were going to have twenty days together. But as a highly knowledgeable engineer and experienced researcher she fired out a succession of questions anyway. To his surprise he found that the girl's charm went far beyond her clothes.

In order to cut short the lively conversation, which seemed to be interesting for the surrounding passengers, he took out a book to read, but it was a challenge to stand up reading on a jolting train. However, his strategy worked and she stopped talking.

She remained silent for a long while. Driven by his rediscovered chivalry, he considered it impolite for a man to focus on a book while ignoring his female counterpart. Coming from a family obsessed with etiquette brought him a lot aggravation indeed. He shifted his eyesight from the book to the girl, only to find her asleep. With her anxiety dispelled by her acquaintance with a fellow traveler willing to take care of every single detail of her trip, she fell right into a sound sleep. She was the kind of person who knew how to get the most out of life. Her thick dark hair was blown wildly about her face by the wind as the train sped along. She wasn't really so attractive, just cute. It occurred to him that she might catch a cold sleeping in the wind and he felt the need to be protective of this delicate girl even though nobody had entrusted him with the duty.

"Hey, wake up," he said gently.

She was sound asleep.

"Comrade." He gave a gentle pat on

her shoulder.

"Have we arrived?" She woke up with a start and her eyes were still sleepy.

"The wind is too strong. You'll get sick."

She smoothed her hair self-consciously. "My name is Deng Anting. An is my nickname. Call me An like everybody else. Don't address me as comrade either, I thought you were talking to someone else. Besides, I'm not working in the office. I'm sort of on vacation. So the word *comrade* sounds too formal and awkward."

The name rang a bell. It was the name of a brilliant designer, but he couldn't bring himself to believe that the sweet young woman could be her. Then and there he developed a fondness for her and once again was positive he had seen the sweet smile and sincere eyes somewhere before.

"You don't look like a Northerner." She gazed at him.

"No?" he was impressed by her cleverness. In fact, he had become a downright Northerner in terms of his appearance and speech, which did not have an accent.

"No, definitely not. I have a hunch you're from Shanghai."

Dawei remained quiet, looking out the window.

Unconsciously the girl began tapping her fingers lightly on the table, but with a restrained force in them.

"Have you taken piano lessons before?" he asked boldly.

"How did you know?" She was taken aback, her eyes still fixed on her fingers. "Did my fingers give it away? I've got long fingers. I can stretch up to nine keys. But unfortunately I wasn't a diligent student. I would haggle with my mother when it was time for practice or set the clock behind, all kinds of tricks, you know. But by the time I'd developed a serious interest in it when I was a bit older, my piano had been taken away. You don't realize what it is to own something valuable until it's gone."

So she had come from a well-to-do family that expected her to learn to play the piano and grow up to be an accomplished woman. The girl reminded him of his childhood neighbor and friend Xiaomei (Little Sister), who had gone to the same school as him from kindergarten right through to their sophomore year at high school. Exactly like Xiao'an, she had long slender fingers and a strong love for the pleasures of life, but was rather needy.

"Is Xiaomei your family nickname?" he suddenly blurted out.

"I'm the youngest in my family and my nickname is Xiao'an. About ten girls in our residential lane adopted Xiaomei as their nickname."

The people of Shanghai are widely recognized for their ingenuity, but they seem to lose their flair when it comes to giving names. For instance, the older son is always called Big Brother and the younger one Little Brother without exception. Girls were Big Sister and Little Sister. Both Xiaomei and Xiao'an were born with silver spoons in their mouths. Before he had lost his innocence, he used to think that girls should be sweet, elegant, and tender to be attractive. That summarized his concept of women. How shallow his thinking had been! Women have more stamina

than men and greater psychological re-
silience. He was ashamed to admit that
he had relied on his wife every step of
the way for the past twelve years, big
man as he was. To achieve more flex-
ibility and toughness, cast iron must
be treated with a high temperature by
being dipped in cold water. The same
process is required of a girl who wishes
to grow into a mother and be worthy of
the ultimate title of "woman." The girl
sitting before him, delicate as a morning glory flower, must be shaped by life
before she could ever expect to be tough
and mature. She might never make it in
the worst-case scenario. His experience
told him that girls like Xiaomei might
for ever remain pampered and dependent and remain spoiled children later
in life. This could be considered fortunate or unfortunate, depending on your

point of view. He had been apart from such specimens for a long time, so long indeed that he thought her kind were already extinct. But the reality is that the Creator is still scattering tons of such seeds around with the lucky ones landing in the fertile land and the unlucky ones falling into the cracks of rocks. Where the seeds land is beyond their control, which may still be the case in a billion years. But the choice of vigorous growth or self-destruction rests with each one of them.

His family had lived on Hunan Road, which was located in an affluent area of Shanghai, dotted with luxurious villas. Dawei lived a carefree life there until he was ten. Being a bridge fan his father indulged in games all day long, to the extent that he started skipping din-

ners at home routinely. However, someone called Uncle Liu became a regular
houseguest, while Dawei's mother was
a housewife. The three of them would
sit at the dinner table like a real family.
Uncle Liu was happy-go-lucky and had
a knack for making people laugh, especially his mother.

But one day a terrible incident
occurred that brought his childhood
innocence to a premature end. The
math teacher had called in sick, and
with the class cancelled the students
were allowed home early. He was so
excited that he dashed all the way home
like a prison inmate released on general
pardon. In order to catch his mother off
her guard, he sneaked into the house,
instead of crashing through the door
in his usual boisterous fashion, but he
found the sitting room empty. Then

he made for his mother's bedroom and gently turned the doorknob in order to surprise her. Upon opening the door, he was horrified to see his mother and Uncle Liu kissing. Ten-year-old boy as he was, he still knew enough to sense something inappropriate was going on. Faced with the sudden intrusion, they withdrew from each other and tried to regain their composure. The young boy was devastated.

At dinner table, Uncle Liu was as cheerful and talkative as ever. But the boy was bitter about the insult to his family and broke down in tears. His mother's face went pale and she was about to give him some comforting pats when Uncle Liu whispered, "It's all right. He's just a kid."

No! He wasn't just a kid. Although he was in no position to judge their behavior, he couldn't tolerate such a remark, or the way his feelings were being ignored.

Next to his home was the small, attractive villa where Xiaomei lived with her family. She had a sister, five years her senior. Five years can be a lifetime to a kid. The older sister acted like an adult. Xiaomei and Dawei were in the same class at kindergarten. He shied away from boys because being weak and meek he couldn't push them around. He could get his way with Xiaomei and was naturally attracted to her company. After getting back from school, he would jump the fence into her yard. He hated ringing the doorbell as he had to greet whoever else was in the house, which he considered a nuisance. Besides, he was often being shepherded out because Xiaomei was busy with homework. He

considered it great fun to jump over
the fence and sneak up on Xiaomei. He
would either read a picture book and
wait until she finished or offer to do it
for her if his patience ran out. Then they
would play games and have a fabulous
time.

Everyone needs somebody to confide
in during the bad times. Dawei found
a sympathetic ear in Xiaomei and got
everything off his chest, including Uncle Liu's remark that he was too young
to understand. The news spread like
wildfire after Xiaomei revealed all to
her mother. One night, his father summoned him to his room and ordered
him to tell him everything he knew. His
father rarely had the patience to talk to
him. Pleased to be listened to at last, he
gave a detailed account of the episode,
feeling a sense of elation as he revealed

the secret.

The following day at breakfast, her eyelids swollen, his mother cast him a pathetic and ashamed look, which he would never forget for the rest of his life. Around three o'clock in the afternoon, he was summoned home from school to be told that his mother had taken her own life by drinking DDT. He was horrified. His statement to his father had been the direct cause of his mother's death. A huge burden weighed heavily on his innocent young soul, and he still hadn't put the guilt behind him.

Six months later his stepmother entered the picture and with her came a lot of changes. To begin with, unlike his own mother, she didn't keep a little light on in the dark narrow hallway which he dreaded passing through each time he came back home late. His fear was rooted in a rumor that someone had committed suicide there before his family moved in. In the past, whenever he was prevented from returning home early for some reason, his mother would leave a light on at night so that he wouldn't be frightened. The light of the lamp was the light of love. He was grateful to his mother for caring so much about him. With his mother's death, the light of love had vanished for good. Fortunately, another light took its place to some extent, that of Xiaomei.

Whenever he felt lonely at night, he would lean over the windowsill, watching Xiaomei's window on the second floor next to his house. A light streamed out of her room and scattered its rays over the oleander tree in front of her window, clothing its leaves with a layer of golden yellow as if in a fairy tale. He would gaze long and hard at her window until her room turned dark.

"Can you keep the light on a little longer?" he once beseeched her.

"Why?"

"To keep me company. I feel so lonely."

"Alright. What time would you like me to turn it off?"

"How about ten o'clock?"

"Sure."

She kept her word. But one night she fell asleep and the light was on the whole night. In the lonely days without maternal love, he was grateful that a flicker of light warmed his heart. Sad and lonely, he yearned for love and company and once he got hold of them he clung on like ivy.

Once she reached high school, Xiaomei found herself rather weak in science subjects, as often happened to pretty girls. It got to the point where she had to take a repeat exam to determine whether she would be able to go on to the next grade. Unwilling to see her drop out of his class, Dawei volunteered to be her tutor and coach her in an attempt to help her pass the exam. However, at such a critical juncture, Xiaomei was far from focused on her studies, remaining the spoiled little girl she had always been.

At that time, something occurred that was to drastically change the course of Dawei's life.

He was in the process of explaining to Xiaomei the experiment conducted by Torricelli to determine one unit of atmospheric pressure being equal to 76 cm of mercury when she suddenly cut him short and said mysteriously,

"Listen, I've learned how to dance after watching the Russian movie *The Melody of Love* five times to study the waltz segment. I've got the hang of it and actually dancing isn't that difficult."

He freaked out. In the sixties, social dance was off limits for middle school students. He had known of two young-sters being detained by the police sta-tion for "dancing in the dark."

"Come on, let me show you." She was a little carried away and put down the blinds and shut the door, knowing full well that what she was doing was ta-boo. She was both nervous and excited. As the light dimmed in the room, she placed a record on the phonograph and then started to move her steps to the music. With the enchanting lyrical mel-ody in the air, her shapely figure swung and swayed as light as a feather.

He was only eighteen then and at that very moment he felt in his heart a tremor he had never experienced before. A ripple of indescribable joy pulsed through his body.

"Come on." She reached out her hand. "Shall we dance? Just follow my steps."

As if by a miracle he was able to keep up his steps to the rhythm unguided. He gingerly held her in his arms as if she were a porcelain doll which might be accidentally crushed to pieces. A sweet and cheerful melody filled the room, bearing cordial wishes; the song *When a Baby Is Born* was to remain etched in his memory for ever.

Suddenly, the door was flung open and Xiaomei's mother uttered a shrill scream that separated them.

That very night, he was dismayed to see her room pitch black.

From then on he felt as if he were contaminated with some persistent dirt he couldn't remove. His neighbors talked about him behind his back; his father kept sighing; and his stepmother and half siblings gloated over his mishap; his teacher forced him to write "self-criticism" without end; the security section of the neighborhood committee summoned him for questioning; and worst of all, to his greatest dismay, the only glimmer of light in his life vanished when Xiaomei moved to another neighborhood and school. He was never again to see the light that would stay on in the night.

Now the tragedy of his mother, a person broken by her circumstances, was almost repeated in him. He would have gone the same way if the mining enterprise from the Northwestern region wasn't recruiting workers in Shanghai.

He couldn't handle another second in the city. His only mistake, if he had committed any, was that he hadn't coached Xiaomei properly. He didn't deserve to be described as "dirty and obscene" and called all the names in the book. Falsehoods become truths if repeated over and over again. He was made to feel like a criminal, low, indecent, and nasty. The pressure on him was such that he was obliged to flee the city to save face.

Ten days after he submitted his application, he left. His father saw him off at the railway station and seemed to think "good riddance" as Dawei boarded the train. Thus his whole life took an unforeseen and drastic turn.

Life is forever a riddle. The desolate, barren Gobi Desert added to the rigor of a life that had already become a misery to him. Many times he woke up in the middle of the night and, hearing his exhausted wife's snoring and the icy cold gusts of wind against the window, he would wonder how different his life would have been if it hadn't been for the song *When a Baby Is Born*. He took pride in being a tough man, tempered by the desert sandstorms, unlike his half siblings who wore nice clothes, fattened up like pigs, and led an indolent and worthless life. Their self-importance was ridiculous to him and their parasitic way of life draining his father's wealth despicable.

When the train arrived, he helped Xiao'an with her traveling bag which felt heavy and hard. What was inside the bag?

"Books. I'm going to apply for graduate school next year. I didn't want to give up the trip to the beach though. I thought I'd better bring the books while I was here."

So she turned out to be fairly diligent and studious. The profile of the future graduate student in a jeans suit struck him as comical.

From a railway station vendor she bought two big watermelons, for which she said her mouth was watering due to a shortage of the fruit in Shanghai that year.

Along the way she told him the story about her whole life without omitting a detail. As he had suspected, she shared Xiaomei's family background more or less. Being the only daughter, she lived in material comfort and was constantly showered with affection and care. Finishing high school in 1974, she was excused from farming in the countryside according to the government policy, which on its own was enough to make him jealous. In 1977 with the national college entrance exam back in place, she was admitted to Shanghai Industrial University with her major in metallurgical engineering and now worked in the Metallurgical Design Institute. What an enviable life, as if God himself had paved the way for her! Little wonder she would say now and then, "Luck always knocks on my door."

"My trip is going to be good, I'm sure of it. It's a good omen meeting you." She was being appreciative again. In a fit of excitement, the two watermelons almost slipped from her grasp. He could never imagine a girl who looked so much like a naughty schoolgirl was going to graduate school. She didn't have anything hard and metallic about her, just a strong feminine essence.

"Why did you go in for metallurgical engineering?"

"Why not?" she gave a sharp retort, unlike her usual abashed and meek self. She was deeply hurt.

"Girls tend to take up foreign language or medical studies. Plus, you look rather delicate."

"So you also think in the same terms about me," she looked discouraged and said. "This is the exact reason why I decided to go in for metallurgy. I love the spectacle of molten iron flowing out of a furnace. A person must be tough and strong to get ahead in life."

He looked at her in disbelief. She went on, "Right across my house lived a woman who was the most fashionably dressed in our lane. She was nicknamed 'UFO' in which U stands for upswept hairdo, F for fancy dress, and O for odd pointed shoes. She walked with confident and graceful steps. I was so impressed that I wanted to grow up overnight and be just like her. However, the other neighbors didn't think much of her outfits or her. One day, I paid a visit to the Shanghai No. 3 Iron and Steel Works on a school trip. A furnace was spitting out molten iron. There was our 'UFO' wearing a safety helmet and an asbestos-insulated jacket, directing the operation with a megaphone while all the male workers followed her orders obediently. She looked so cool and glamorous. I never expected her to be a metallurgical engineer overseeing operations at a blast furnace. Every young girl has an idol, and she was mine. I was about thirteen then, but I knew that a woman must possess both beauty and learning, like her. I wanted to have the same upswept hairdo as I oversaw blast furnaces when I grew up ..." She chuckled. "The hairdo is past its sell by date, but my dream has come true. At the time I didn't know metallurgical engineering had so many subspecialties. When I was assigned to doing designs I was disappointed that I would never make it to the blast furnaces with a megaphone."

"That project of yours was quite challenging to you, I suppose," he said, convinced now that she was the project designer.

"That was a project I worked on in my final year. I spent seven solid months on it, no days off, no movies, only work."

"You have a strong will."

"Thanks for the compliment, but Aunt Zhang, the one I saw as a teenager, she was the one with a strong will. During the Cultural Revolution, her hair was shaved off on one side, but she bought a wig at City God Temple, striding in and out of the lane as usual. In 1976 she was diagnosed as having stomach cancer and three-fourths of her stomach was removed. Days after leaving the hospital, she was back at the blast furnace with her megaphone. Her shoes were round-headed though, instead of being pointed; and her hair cropped short, instead of being upswept. Most people thought she was getting too old to fuss about her appearance, but I loved to see her dressed up to the nines. I think a person should not only make herself outwardly attractive, but also accomplish something tangible ... What's so funny? Am I talking nonsense?"

"Oh, no, what you said makes perfect

sense. You certainly have the right kind of values."

"Values? Ever since I was old enough to know about life, I've kept reminding myself to grow up as tough and capable as Aunt Zhang, rather than an old-fashioned woman."

"But where's Aunt Zhang?"

"She's dead. But she knew I had been enrolled in a university metallurgy program. She's a real heroine to me still. She said she wasn't afraid of death and that only those who had accomplished nothing in their lifetime were. For all the twists and turns imaginable, she managed to make her life a success ..."

"What she said is absolutely true." Dawei kept nodding his approval and admired the woman engineer for her keen insight into life.

"But I fear death, because I haven't

seen the world yet." The girl lost her composure and looked disturbed.

"Well, you're still young and the days ahead are long and arduous. You'll have your share of tough experiences in life," he said seriously.

"As a matter of fact, I ..." she halted in the middle of her sentence and let out a deep sigh.

Something seemed to be bothering her. The cheerful, carefree princess was not immune from human worries and anxieties.

Chapter 2

"Why are you sticking so close to me all the time?" he asked Xiao'an.

"Because I feel a sense of security when I'm with you. You're so big and strong that nothing could crush you," she said admiringly.

"What do you think might crush you?"

"I really don't know." She forced a smile. "He said I'm like a morning glory flower that sticks to whatever it catches and won't let it go."

"Who are you talking about?"

"A friend of mine, a former class-mate." She blushed.

It dawned on him that what was bothering her was the torment of love, which was a sweet torment, a game which cute girls like her might get caught up in. As far as some women were concerned, they had never experienced such a game. For instance, his wife, woman as she was, had missed too many things regarded as sweet and fun in life.

"Would you say the morning glory is no good because it's too dependent?" she asked tentatively. The girl gave the false impression that working high at the designer's desk, pencil and triangular ruler in hand, she would churn out things like Cupid's arrows, rather than a blueprint that involved tedious math calculations and straight and curved lines. How could a sophisticated design project and a morning glory flower, two such incompatible things, both find their way into one and the same girl? Probably it would be better to keep the outlandish combination so that metal would be given a feminine appeal.

"I think you're lovelier than a morning glory flower," he assured her, thinking then of Xiaomei, who had also been in the habit of clinging to him like a little bird. She often worried about things like quarterly tests, sudden quizzes, end of term exams, etc., etc., and bugged him about guessing test items, coaching, and copying notes. In the company of such a girl, he felt manly.

But not all men love to mix with girls who are sweet, soft, and pampered. Take himself for instance. He preferred a coarse, capable, and hardworking woman like his wife. In the course of many years' close association with her, he developed a preference for a woman of her physical stamina, strongly built, unselfish, and industrious. Each time his wife's robust and diligent figure came into his mind, he was filled with mingled feelings of love and guilt. He felt that, as a husband, he hadn't fulfilled his duty to provide for her so she wouldn't have to do men's work. She took odd jobs at the mine, such as pushing a cart, or making adobe bricks. In spite of her excellent work, she remained a temp. It pained him to see her engaged in backbreaking labor that was meant for men. Several times, seeing her soaked in sweat, he was on the point of giving her a sympathetic kiss. But he checked himself. His wife always treated him like a chick in need of the mother hen's comforting wing, as if he couldn't survive without her protection, despite his muscular build. He didn't want to wound her sense of pride, which needed to be respected and treasured. Just as he found his own value in the path he took through life, so his wife found hers in the way she was treated by her husband. What she delivered was not only tender love as a wife, but also the maternal affection, which he had lost too soon. A pretty face was incapable of giving such love, whether Xiaomei or Xiao'an.

As if transmitted by an electrical brain wave, Xiao'an asked gently, "Does your better half also cling to you?"

"You're talking about my wife?" He wasn't used to the fashionable expression *better half*. "She's mentally and physically strong, not a morning glory. A flower has no chance of survival in the Gobi Desert."

"Is she ... pretty?"

That was what women were usually inquisitive about.

"No."

"But you're handsome." Her straightforward comment made him self-conscious.

"Physical beauty is of little importance in a relationship."

"It sounds true. An English proverb goes: 'Love is blind' and a Chinese equivalent saying goes something like this: 'Beauty is in the eye of the beholder.'"

But things may look more complex in real life. A pretty face is part of beauty which is the sum of parts. Beauty brings about love which in turn perfects beauty.

He remembered a girl student in

his high school class, who had a very
cute face with a clean-cut outline that
resembled the plaster bust on the art
teacher's desk. But he hated her because
of her sharp tongue, shrewdness, and
cunning. She would argue with her
teacher in order to boost her test score
by one or two points, to the extent of
faking a correct answer. At the meeting
held for his "wrongdoing," she tightened
her pretty face and launched a volley
of horrendous remarks through her
sensuous red lips, such as "the influence
of the exploiting class," "the corrosion
of bourgeois thinking," etc. etc. She was
like the wicked queen in *Snow White*. He
would never be interested in a woman
like that.

"How eloquent!" she flattered him.
"You possess a poet's sensitivity and
insight. You undoubtedly could be a

writer if you wanted to."

He smiled and thought he had merely expressed what he had learned from life. Regrettably, his life was anything but poetic and his love encounter as un-romantic as the five worn fingers on his hand. He had started the search for his life companion when "beauty" was not a word in his vocabulary. He was too busy with beating a trail through the jungle of life. What he had in mind was a reliable and supportive partner committed to his titanic effort. Whether that woman was beautiful or not mattered little to him and in fact a pretty face was as illusory as a desert mirage. In his eyes, his wife was beautiful although she wasn't a gorgeous rose or a ravishing peony. She was beautiful in her own way and he had married the most beautiful woman in the world.

One time the sheep pen had collapsed in a snowstorm, injuring his leg. For the next six months his wife carried him on her broad back to the clinic for treatment twice a week. As she struggled along he felt awkward and helpless, so awful in fact that he was about to curse and slap himself. During the time on his wife's back he discovered on her neck a rosy mole resembling the red dot, or bindi, on an Indian woman's forehead. He had never noticed her incredibly white soft skin before. She looked stunning with the red ruby birthmark set on the back of her slender neck. Each time as he lay on her back, he would stare lovingly at the rosy mole thinly covered with locks of her hair. One time he couldn't resist the temptation and kissed the mole. She jerked her head around, frightened, but with gleaming tears of happiness mixed with her sweat. That scene was burned on his memory like a perfect photograph. It would remain in his mind even when she turned into a stooping white-haired old lady leaning on a stick or after she was long gone. In his mind's eye he saw once again the smiling woman whose face was covered with tears and sweat. Life was tough, but beautiful too. It was worth living with all its thorns. But this kind of philosophy was beyond the carefree Xiao'an.

Xiao'an clung to him like a morning glory flower with all its entwined vines, and saw him as her own protector. On the pretext of a small appetite she would slip to him under the table the steamed bread, which was not her favorite. But she was in a dilemma when she sometimes came across her favorite food; for instance, the Tianjian Go Believe buns, which she was served one day but slipped to him with a reluctant heart. This situation greatly amused him.

"I guess you can handle this particular kind of flour food. Save it for yourself," he whispered, slipping the buns back to her.

"Thank you." She took her buns back without a moment's hesitation, casting a furtive look at him. For a second, he grew jealous of her. She had everything: an easy life, youthful energy, good looks, and a promising career. In comparison, his wife had nothing. Even the steamed buns made of enriched flour which Xiao'an hated were a luxury for her. His envy faded, however, when she smiled her charming smile again. Her cheerful personality was an example for all women.

But life wasn't all plain sailing for Xiao'an. He would often find her eyes puffy and red in the morning. She routinely went to the post office to check her mail. He hoped that it was nothing too serious. It seemed to him that sooner or later she would pour her heart to him, but he had reservations about it. Love problems weren't really his cup of tea. He had no idea how young people thought about love, and so had no advice to offer her, he dreaded looking awkward when the moment came.

One day he lost control and yelled at her. Shame on a big man like him yelling at a little girl! To fly into a rage was a particularly heinous thing to do on a calm, serene sea shore, where vacationers were basking under the scorching sunshine with an insatiable greed for a tanned skin. He couldn't figure out how he had got into such a fit of temper under the azure blue sky.

That day he had been lying on the burning hot sand, his leg aching from the old injury. He buried it and felt a soothing sensation relieving the dull pain. Xiao'an was stretched out on the sand, waking up from a pleasant nap.

"Did I doze off?" She sat up and rubbed her eyes. With her skin deeply tanned, she looked great.

"Oh, no!" she suddenly cried.

"What happened?"

"I looked pretty disgusting sleeping with my mouth hanging open, didn't I?"

He couldn't stand her peculiar way of thinking.

Some dandelions were floating in front of her and she grabbed one.

"You know, my boyfriend likes the song '*I am a dandelion seed and whither I go I do not know ...*' But I know where it goes. Now here is the rest of the song." She improvised with a mischievous smile.

"Hey, you Shanghai guy,
You are like a dandelion seed.
As the wind blows,
You land in the Gobi Desert.
How do you survive all these years?
And don't you want to return to Shanghai?"

Finishing the song, she threw a consoling look at him. It reminded him of Mr T-shirt's condescension, this time coming from none other than the girl under his protection. True he didn't have a Shanghai residence card, but he didn't appreciate the little doll's sympathy. In the eyes of the Shanghainese, he looked

boorish and provincial, which was due
to the ordeal of sleeping in a bunker for
five years and eating nothing but corn
bread. He contracted edema in 1963.
His face had swollen to the point of
transparency, the mere press of a finger
causing large dints in the skin. Back
in the good old days in Shanghai his
breakfast had consisted of a glass of milk,
a hard-boiled egg, plus four pieces of
buttered toast with jam. After breakfast,
his mother would force a spoonful of
thick and smelly cod liver oil down his
throat in order to keep him energized.
After his mother's death, the cod liver
oil ritual had finished. However, he was
still fed a large breakfast as before, up to
the very morning he boarded the train
north. But now he had forgotten the
taste of butter. He was able to swallow
without a grunt the bitter pills life had

offered him. He was a child no more.
Everybody had edema. What was the
big fuss? In the days when the mining
area was nothing but a stretch of barren
land, he and his starving fellow workers
hauled their first piece of machinery
into place with merely ropes slung over
their shoulders. "The Shanghai boy is
incredible!" They patted him on the
shoulder. Letting it go to his head, he
marveled at his limitless energy and
vitality. The tender seedling that had
sprouted on the Shanghai asphalt had
now struck deep roots in the Gobi
Desert! He had made it! That was why
he was upset to find himself an object of
pity and ridicule. His outburst stunned
her and the other tourists as well. It
was quite a while before she walked
away, her head hung low, bursting into
a convulsion of sobs.

He continued to lie on the sand, but with a sour taste in his mouth. He had savagely ripped away the tender vines clinging to him. Without a generous heart, how could he consider himself a man? Why should he even care what others thought about his life as long as he himself believed he was on the right path?

He looked towards the blue sky which was clear and bright as if washed clean by the waters of the sea. On the horizon were colorful sailing boats piloted by sun-tanned, boisterous boys and girls busy posing. But they were intoxicated more with the pleasure of controlling the vessel than with their posturing. It was hard to believe that a beach full of so much vitality and a vast desolate desert existed side by side, probably as a result of what geologists called "ecological balance." Land is balanced by water, the tropical zone by the frigid zone, Star Sea Beach by the great Gobi Desert, smiles by tears. If it was really that way he should be courageous enough to face reality and prove himself to be a man worth his salt. He had heard a lot about "fulfilling social commitments." Society had commitments, which it expected its citizens to fulfill for the sake of others. Thanks to socially conscious people like Dawei, Xiao'an was able to live an easy life. As these thoughts crossed his mind, he was filled with remorse for the outburst that had obviously deeply hurt her.

Someone came over to announce that the tour bus was ready to take them to a nearby scenic spot called Dragon Mountain and that it would leave in fifteen minutes. This was a good opportunity for him to make up with Xiao'an. However, he didn't find her on the bus or anywhere around. She must be crying somewhere. Once a girl got upset, it would take her a long time to shake it off. At Dragon Mountain, vendors were selling seashell necklaces. He got one for her, thinking of the dispute that had occurred between them earlier in the day. He felt bad about the episode that had spoiled their trip to the beach. Hotdogs were served for lunch and despite her absence he was given her portion.

Back at the hotel, he got ready for dinner, feeling tense. As he apprehensively stepped into the restaurant, he found the seat next to hers vacant, wondering whether it was saved for him or not. She was her usual smiling, cheerful self when she showed up; her eyes sparkling with excitement, with no trace of her earlier distress. He looked defeated over another error of judgment on his part.

As she slipped her steamed bread to him under the table as usual, he held her hand for a moment as a sign of apology on his part. She seemed to have put the incident behind her. With her face lighting up, she said, "Do you know where I have been to today? To a local steel plant. I learned from the hotel attendant Little Gao that the plant was going to test and adopt my unit. Little Gao's brother happens to be working there and I asked him to take me to the site." Fixing the seashell necklace on her sun-tanned neck, she babbled on, "This is the first time I've seen my design as a finished product. I was bombarded with questions after

they found out who I was. Someone
made me uneasy even by addressing
me respectfully as 'Ms. Deng.' I looked
cool, just like Aunt Zhang. They had
prepared everything for me, from the
hard hat to the insulation jacket, but
no megaphone ... Sadly, Shanghai is
full of talented people who get taken
for granted. But here you are somebody
treated with respect and consulted for
professional opinions. I'm still worried
my unit might run into a hitch and fail
though, later on ..." She bit her lips
nervously.

He assured her that her fears were
groundless, as every design had been
meticulously thought out and certified.

"You're right," she said, "but I'm just
nervous, like in my school days when I
used to worry about exam results and
wouldn't relax until I got my report

card."

"I'm sorry your school days still haunt you."

"By no means. I love exams, they help you set goals, give you a chance to evaluate yourself, and give you a fair grade." She was flushed, eyes gleaming.

She was far from weak and vulnerable, he concluded. A tremendous force lay dormant inside her and would erupt some day. It was incredible that she kept her remarkable inner potential hidden with hardly a trace. It wasn't easy to see her as she truly was, despite his penetrating eye.

Chapter 3

The conference was drawing to a close and everybody was seizing the last few days to enjoy themselves in one way or another at the beautiful beach where the weather was so pleasant and agreeable. The controversy over a human being born with a good heart versus a wicked heart has remained inconclusive ever since it was initiated. It might be more appropriate to say a human is born with a jolly heart, a desire to seek sunshine and joy. The conference participants were busy making preparations to throw a ball to have a splendid time, which revealed that the engineers otherwise buried in drafts, blueprints, and researches also had a vivacious and vibrant side in their personalities. Even some gray-haired senior engineers were turned on by the event.

"Do you dance?" Xiao'an asked him excitedly.

"No, I hate it." He was touched on the raw. Dancing was for him a distant past, an anathema which he tried not to discuss. He had never expected the arrival of such a day when Western music blared and people danced freely without shutting down the doors and windows. What a difference it would have made to his life if the old days had been like the golden age today!

As night fell, the ballroom was thronged with participants, but he slipped out to the beach to avoid the crowd, including Xiao'an who had been eagerly looking forward to the ball. He didn't want to dampen the girl who was as enthusiastic as he was indifferent.

The nightly beach was breathtaking, the sky clear and bright, all quiet, and the sands lightly touched by the sea tide. In the fuzzy darkness he caught sight of a blurry figure walking along the beach. It was Xiao'an. He couldn't understand why a girl as happy as a lark was now wandering in solitude in the night.

"What's going on, Xiao'an? Are you homesick? ..." he shut up at the sight of tears trickling down her cheeks.

"He doesn't write to me. I've sent him three letters without receiving a single reply from him ..." She sobbed. So she was being tormented by love. Sad as she was, she showed no sign of being lovelorn. Instead, she looked more like a little girl grabbing for candies, unabashedly and without concealing her inner self. Her boyfriend had every reason to feel fortunate to have such a pure and innocent soul, rather than give her a hard time.

"For twenty days he hasn't written to me."

"He should know better than to keep you waiting."

"Oh, no. He loves me," she threw him a cold look, quick to come to his defense. The childish girl was really in need of some counseling.

"Or he may be too busy to write to you."

"Absolutely not," she shook her head dejectedly. "I guess the reason is he loves too well, but not wisely. He's from out of town. And he's not a native of Shanghai, without a residence card!" So that was that. He tried to figure why she had fallen in love with someone other than a Shanghainese.

"I met him for the first time in Dalian where I was a student intern. It was also a night at the beach like this ... Hmm, maybe someone of your age will never understand our relationship. Although we live apart and speak different dialects, we couldn't resist falling in love."

Someone of my age? Dawei suppressed a laugh, thinking he wasn't that old yet.

"That night, we stood by the sea, enjoying the view of the horizon. Oh, by the way, do you know the story *Red Sail*? It's about a sailboat flying a red sail. As the boat looms up at the horizon, the young man stands firm in his boat. Gradually the mast of the boat drifts into view. Finally he is here ..."

It was a fantastic story. Only young people were capable of weaving their sweet dreams into such a tale. Holding her hand in his own, he encouraged her to go on.

"But, I'm a bad woman and don't deserve the young man in the boat. I was supposed to marry a guy mother had chosen for me on National Day this year ..."

It might sound ludicrous, but it is true. Girls of Xiaomei's breeding were confined to their cozy nests and treated like pretty porcelain dolls in a showcase. Loving but unwise parents put high price tags on them and shifted them from one gleaming showcase to another. The cold showcase glass cut them off from fresh air and reality, so they continued living in a utopian, transcendental vacuum. The villas in his neighborhood had been filled with porcelain dolls like these. They sometimes recoiled from the arrangement, and he knew too well what they were unhappy about.

"Why didn't you marry him? I guess it's not something an ambitious girl like you would do."

"Stop making fun. I genuinely felt I had never stepped beyond the confines of my house until my internship started. I went through the Cultural Revolution, but it did little to unshackle me. You know what kind of boys were thrust upon me? A bunch of meek, white-skinned sucklings. They looked like something kneaded out of enriched flour. Some of them shared a similar family background and level of education, but were pressed on me by their parents and I felt pissed about it. I may not look great, but I yearn for someone who shares my belief in love for the sake of love.

"I couldn't go on endlessly waiting for my dream boat to arrive. I was in danger of being left on the shelf. That was when my mother stepped in. Actually, he was a nice guy and we were a good match in many ways, family, education, you know. But he just didn't turn me on. I thought I would change and fall in love as time went by."

So that was how the boy from Dalian entered the picture and made such a ripple in her life, overwhelming her with waves of love and passion. But in the case of marriage in China, the main issue was practicality. The problems of legal residential status and the rationing cooking oil and staple food that came with it would become serious in years to come. The dream for which tremendous sacrifices had been made would eventually vanish like a burst bubble. Was it worth it? At one time he had had a sweet dream, too, that involved a light shining in his neighbor Xiaomei's window and an oleander tree glistening like gold. The light and the tree had for a long while remained a part of his life. He never made any attempt to recover the lost dream, though. Life had made him believe that such an attempt would prove futile. The dream, however poetic, would lose its glamour and charm if reality was allowed to intrude.

"I had my share of beautiful dreams in my youth, too."

He decided to tell her all about his past for her to draw some lessons from. He started to look back on the footprints he had left behind him, whether firm or weak, straight or meandering. Every footprint had its special meaning for him.

"She was my childhood friend. I came from a well-to-do family that lived in Hunan Garden. It was an affluent area of Shanghai at the time ..." he adopted a calm tone in narrating his life story.

She listened attentively, but interrupted him when he mentioned his mother's suicide, "Was she pretty?"

"Quite."

"But you bear a grudge against her, don't you?" she said seriously.

"She has my sympathy." He was vaguely aware as a kid that Uncle Liu was his mother's lover, but couldn't afford to marry her as he had been unemployed for a lengthy period of time.

"So your mother was trapped in a loveless marriage. She deserved sympathy." Xiao'an flinched at the stinging cold. "But she has some responsibility; I mean she shouldn't have agreed to get married in the first place."

"But it was arranged by her father who took the matter into his own hands."

"Oh?" she let out a sigh. Throwing her hair back, she decided to change the subject.

"You haven't been to Shanghai for a long time, have you? It's still your home town."

"What do I care when nobody there cares about me? I don't miss Shanghai. Anyway, I paid a visit last year, the first time in years. Sometimes I can be a bit fragile."

He laughed. Some things in life defy explanation. When his life had become relatively stable and he had got the education he wanted, he was seized by a strong desire to see the city he had left twenty years before. In the dead of night scenes from his past flashed across his mind. The thriving Huaihai Road, the multi-flavored dried horse beans of City God Temple, the popsicle hawker's hollering in the streets on hot summer days, and above all his childhood home, the villa, which he now had no ties with. The house had been returned to his stepmother and half siblings who had been evicted during the Cultural Revolution. When he left Shanghai, he had gone into a self-imposed exile of humiliation and agony. After he had created a new life for himself, he yearned to return for a visit, not to rub people's noses in his success, but to win respect and admiration from his native city. So when a new policy was announced, allowing state employees to visit their birth places once every four years, he had got himself a train ticket right away and set off on the long overdue trip.

On the platform at Shanghai station, returning passengers were warmly hugged and kissed by those who had come to meet them. An unlikely hope rose in his heart, the hope of spotting in the welcoming crowd a familiar face, even if it was that of his stepmother or one of his half siblings. He swore he was ready, if one of them showed up, to bury the hatchet and start over. He kept looking around hopefully, but nobody came to meet him.

The city was less than enthusiastic in its response to his return. His stepmother was neither cordial nor cold, just cool. The streets and boulevards welcomed him with open arms, but the shop assistants looked suspiciously at him because of his rough leather boots and scruffy clothes. He felt like a square peg in a round hole when he mixed with the fashionably dressed city dwellers. There was a big gap between the city he had remembered and the city as it had become. Cream-coated dried horse beans were no longer the exclusive product of City God Temple, but they had lost their rich flavor. Popsicles had given way to ice cream brick to cater to more sophisticated palates. He was baffled as well as disappointed to find that Shanghai didn't hold as great a spell as he had imagined it would. The change in his appearance brought about by years of hard living was such that his in-laws treated him like an outsider and tried to add a Northern twist to the Mandarin they spoke to him. For his part, he looked at his courteous and sickly pale friends with pity. A man worth his salt needed to be tempered and toughened by the storms of life. Only then could he show off the lines etched across his forehead. He felt great walking the familiar streets in his coarse leather boots, not giving a damn about what others thought of him. He had left as a loser, but returned as a man, a proud but injured warrior back from the battlefront. "I love you, Shanghai."

However, an incident occurred that completely ruined his trip. A distant relative of his father's was coming back to Shanghai for a visit and his fawning stepmother managed to get him to stay at her house for three days. In order to put up the new guest, she asked Dawei to move out of the big room where he was staying into the small storage room. She even asked him to disappear for a few days "for the sake of the country." She fretted about their American relative walking away with an bad impression of the Tang family because of one shabbily dressed "black sheep." That was the last straw for him.

"I'll leave as soon as I get a train ticket," he said angrily. His belated return had rapidly gone to hell.

The villa that had once been home now gave him an uncomfortable and eerie feeling. Life in this house was diametrically opposed to the values of society. Surely he was nothing compared with the classy Shanghainese. But as a man of honor he had earned every penny he had the hard way. Here in the house, freeloading was seen as something honorable and hard work treated with disdain. And his in-laws were mean enough to keep a constant eye on him, thinking he had returned to Shanghai with ideas about reclaiming family property.

"Nobody there cares about me," he said with a long sigh. "There's no sense going back." He forced a smile.

"What about that little girl? You haven't seen her since, have you?" she asked. "They say people fall in love only once in their lifetime. Is that how it is with you?"

While her concept of love was found in sentimental novels, he had his own ideas. He didn't read novels. From the time his life became one of sleeping in a bunker and chewing vegetables, he had harbored a strong dislike for love stories. The authors, divorced from reality, churned out tedious rubbish. They should at least have had a taste of his lifestyle before taking up their pens. All the same, his childhood dream still lingered in his memory and remained indestructible, despite a life of hardship and privation, until the trip to Shanghai.

He had done a quite stupid thing during

his stay in Shanghai. In the garden of Xiaomei's house a magnolia tree stood in place of the oleander tree that used to face her bedroom. The oleander tree had been pulled up by the roots in a typhoon. The soft light still flickered through the window, but it wasn't Xiaomei's any more. His strong yearning for the pretty but unscholarly Xiaomei didn't seem to result from love, but nostalgia. She was another symbol of past luxury, his milk-and-toast breakfast ritual, all those unchanging daily routines; an attractive golden lining for the layers of beautiful memories in his head.

He had no trouble finding information about the whereabouts of Xiaomei's family. They lived in an English-style apartment building on Changle Road, not far from their former residence. So for the last twenty years she was a stone's throw from his house.

Xiaomei hadn't changed much, although it took some time before she was able to recognize him. When he saw the dusty footprints left by his coarse boots on the shining hardwood floor and heard a few groans of protest from the sofa springs under his heavy weight, he regretted his rash decision to call on her.

But Xiaomei was delirious about his visit.

"I'm sorry I still can't figure out Torricelli's experiment." She blinked her eyes mischievously. In an instant he felt as if he was seeing the girl as she was, but only for a brief second. "No one can predict what's going to happen in future, right? Last Saturday, we threw a family ball and danced until midnight. You were too naïve then, no, we were too naïve."

"Without that incident, I would have

left home anyway. It was a matter of time," he said firmly after pausing a few seconds and bit his thumb.

"Not necessarily," she disagreed. "For two years in a row I failed in the college entrance exam following high school graduation. The neighborhood committee took turns trying to talk me into going to the Northwest. I totally ignored them. During the Cultural Revolution they repeated their drama to send me to an island farm near Shanghai. But I stuck it out. You see, it worked!"

Obviously she failed to catch his point. She didn't understand his predicament.

"What are you doing now?"

"I used to work in a neighborhood processing plant. But I quit. It's not worth it slaving for forty-five yuan a month."

Not worth it? His wife still hadn't turned regular and her brother was almost driven to suicide for failure to earn a fixed income of forty yuan a month.

The reunion fell flat like the one between the estranged Paul and Tonya in a previous Soviet novel popular in China in the early fifties. He wasn't a staunch revolutionary like Paul, but he wasn't a loser, weak and vulgar, either. There might be lucky and unlucky seeds in the world. But he didn't think of Xiaomei as being a lucky seed. She wasn't even a flower in a green house; she was at best an attractive elaborately-made imitation flower, without luster and vitality. She had never been exposed to the real world, not knowing the joy of a sprouting seed, the nurture of dews, or the solace of sunshine.

After a brief ceremonious exchange of words, they fell silent, but gazed at each other, trying to recall the sweet childhood memory through the windows of eyes and the inscrutable veil of life. Both of them made a futile attempt due to the unfathomable abyss between them.

At parting, he was on the point of asking her whether she still remembered the song *When a Baby Is Born*. But he held his tongue for fear of spoiling the last remaining trace of the sweet feelings in his heart.

"Therefore, in my opinion, reunion between former lovers tends to spoil the perfect image that remains intact in their minds for the reason people change," he said while rubbing his hands nervously. He was seldom sentimental and felt ashamed to give his inner feelings away.

"That means you've never fallen in profound love again," she found her voice after being silent for a few seconds and heaved a sigh.

"It's not true. There has never been true love between me and Xiaomei. As I said, our relationship is one of looking back on our youthful days with a fond memory. It's a mixed feeling. For true love there doesn't exist the question of being profound or shallow. How can I put it? Take my hands. I love them too well to admire or think of applying lotion to protect them. I need them and won't feel complete without them and they are part of me."

"So that's how you treat and love your wife." She was green with envy.

"Yes, although you may think it's a kind of crooked love, not poetic as the *Red Sail* or romantic as *The Cinderella*. But I feel gratified and she deserves being well treated."

It was true his wife was different from the image of the perfect woman he had in mind when he was younger. She didn't have sweet smiles or tender feelings; nor did she have a slender figure or tapering fingers. But her rough powerful hands smoothed the wounds in his heart that had been caused by the loss of maternal love and family support. A rugged woman, she shared with him the heavy family burden, which no other woman could. With her coarse calloused hands, she had lit up an undying light for him. Knowing his significant half was waiting for his return with a tender and eager heart, he grinned with gratification. Life was worth living.

More than ten years ago, while going down the mine shaft in the pitch dark elevator one day, he heard a faint groan:

"I'm going to pass out. Help! Help!" It was a woman's voice. Traditionally, women weren't allowed to work in the mine, supposedly because they would bring bad luck if they were. It was more out of concern for women than superstition though. The work was too tough for women to bear.

"I can't wait any longer. I'm going to throw up."

The next second he heard sounds of vomiting.

"Who's she?" he whispered to someone. "Who sent her down?"

"Big Old Li's daughter. She took over her father's job as her brother is too young."

Big Old Li was the one that plunged to his death last month when the wires hauling the shaft elevator had broken. He was a Korean War veteran who returned in 1952 and the leader of the operation team Dawei was assigned to when he first came to the mining town, but he didn't have a favorable impression of his boss who struck him as skinny and small, uneducated and rough, and didn't look like a soldier who had been involved in real battles before. Yet he was known as "Big" Old Li. Dawei felt superior to his team leader because he was a high school graduate, who knew about Beethoven and Pushkin. It was anybody's guess how much learning the dwarf had "in his belly." Dawei was still full of youthful arrogance and complacency. Coming from Shanghai with the kudos of a high school education, he wasn't inclined to follow his team leader's orders. His life in the mining town was tough beyond description at first. But in the sixties, people generally had enormous push and drive and an indomitable will. He was confident he would outperform everybody else and to prove himself he would find heavy work to do, even though Big Old Li, who didn't have much patience with him, often assigned to him light work that he thought to be fit for girls, such as making adobe bricks. He had an attitude and evaded his team leader's instructions at every turn in one way or another.

That day he was assigned a painting job which he considered a girl's job.

"Be sure to wear gloves or you'll get burned."

"I'll be OK." Dawei assumed a nonchalant attitude. Without the protection of the gloves, his hands were smeared with paint, which was a big mistake. When he called it a day, his hands started hurting and he felt like vomiting.

"Look at my hands." He ruefully showed his red burning hot hands to his friends at dinner.

"I told you! But you wouldn't listen," Big Old Li said to him coldly as he passed by. Dawei couldn't take his snipping and felt like throwing a few punches at the receding figure, but he knew better than that.

That night, Big Old Li paid a visit to him in his dorm, bringing four fresh eggs which were quite a treat in the sixties when famine gripped the nation. He got hold of an aluminum mug, cracked two eggs, and made soup for him. He said in a serious but concerned voice, "We folks at the mine are too busy to take care of you. You're an adult and should learn to live an independent life." His swollen eyes stared at him.

Dawei was grateful as well as embarrassed to take the piping hot egg soup, aware that the eggs purchased by Big Old Li's wife out of her concern for her husband would end up in a stranger's stomach.

"Come on, help yourself. After all you're still a kid and you're growing and you need nourishment. Life is just beginning for you." Big Old Li pressed him to eat and then rose to leave and as he did so a shadow, nice and big, was projected on the rough adobe wall by a stream of light. Now he realized why he was fondly nicknamed "Big" Old Li.

In late 1962, Big Old Li's families were at the end of their resources in their home village. With two children, his wife went and sought refuge with him. In this newly developed mining town in the middle of the poverty-stricken Gansu Province, it was relatively easy to find some odd jobs to do and make some petty cash, which was impossible back in the village and which was essential for the dependants. Besides, the mine was short of hands. So they decided to settle down. His two kids were a pitiful sight, all skin and bones with yellow thin hair, which betrayed their malnutrition. On these heart-rending scenes, Dawei couldn't bear the thought of taking the four eggs out of the couple of hungry mouths; at the same time he was disgusted with his stepmother in Shanghai who discarded the crust to eat the crumb.

Soon afterwards, he was promoted to a welder's position and left Big Old Li's operation team and Li himself was transferred to the pits down the mine. As a result, they saw little of each other. But he never expected that Big Old Li was to die on the job for the sake of the mine.

Four hundred meters down the shaft,

the elevator pulled up and out stepped a big girl with an ashen white face. She wore a roomy jumpsuit and a pair of half-worn athletic shoes with a small white fabric flower pinned in her hair. Although ostensibly taken on to replace her father, the girl was engaged in a different type of job. She was responsible for serving tea to the miners in the pits and was not on the official payroll due to the temporary nature of the work.

Although he had reached marrying age, it was difficult to find the right girl in a place where women were scarce and choice limited. For the plain looking tea girl he only had a sympathetic heart and soon afterwards put her out of his mind, although he continued to enjoy the hot tea she served. He demanded flawless beauty, forgetting the irony that he was too poor to marry.

He knew the time had come for him to have a family. But he was still obsessed with Xiaomei whose image as well as the image of the fantastic golden oleander tree was hard to erase from his mind. His first love experience kept coming back to him. Living in the vast desolate desert dotted with only white poplar and sand jujube trees instead of oleander trees, he fervently hoped that Xiaomei's figure would some day appear in front of him. When he reached the age of thirty, he finally realized how ludicrous it was to live on a hope that would never materialize. But he wouldn't give up and continued to live a fantasy until someone snapped him out of it and fixed him up with a Guangxi girl who was an accountant. The girl was plain looking and being less than handsome himself, he couldn't afford to be picky and made a commitment there and then. But in his heart of hearts he felt it wrong to let himself off so lightly. So he made an excuse to get away from the matchmaker and slipped alone into the little woods where withered leaves were falling and cool autumnal wind blowing, which was typical October weather in Gansu. He stuck to the promise he had made at the age of thirty, a little prematurely, that he would never fall in love again. He treated the marriage deal with less than enthusiasm, even finding himself unable to recall what the Guangxi girl looked like. Yet that was the girl, not Xiaomei, he was going to spend the rest of his life with. If it was never to be with Xiaomei, why not marry any girl? Farewell, Xiaomei! Farewell, the fantastic oleander tree! He rested his head on a tree stump, tears rolling down his face.

"How did the matchmaking go?" she asked with interest when serving hot tea to him the next day.

"It's none of your business!" He was so moody that he scattered all over the floor what was left in the mug and then threw it into the disinfectant, causing it to splash on her. She suffered a tearful night afterwards, as she later confided to him when they were married.

The very same day he withdrew from the bank all of his savings, totaling five hundred and fifty yuan, to be spent on his wedding. The bride-to-be had demanded woolen yarns, a woolen overcoat, leather shoes ... the works. He didn't blame her. Marriage provided her with an once-in-a-lifetime chance to buy herself some decent clothes. A squandered chance never comes back again. Besides, the early seventies were a period of deprivation.

Passing the mine hospital, he saw a crowd of people, the sounds of wailing coming from behind them. The next minute, the crowd parted to make way for two men carrying a door with a boy on it, the lower half of his body a repulsive mass of blood and flesh. Before he was able to figure out who the boy was, he saw Big Old Li's wife and daughter follow in his wake crying.

"Come back. You come back." The doctor wearing his white gown ran after them panting. He grabbed the door and cried, "The massive open wounds are likely to get infected and he could die."

"We appreciate your kindness, Doctor. But we have no insurance. Let him die at home." Big Old Li's wife sobbed and urged the two men to keep walking.

"Cut that out. He's too young to die. We must save him," Dawei shouted, clutching the door handle and pressing into her hand a bunch of banknotes fresh from the bank.

"No, I can't ..."

"Take it. Life is nothing without hope for the future," he comforted her. It was a comfort for himself as well that as long as he stuck around he would sooner or later find the right girl to marry.

Several days later he found Big Old Li's daughter back with her tea bucket.

"Back to work? How's your brother doing?"

"He's fine, thank you," she smiled and said with relief. "The doc said he was of tough constitution and that's why he survived." Her face darkened. "But he's lost one of his legs."

"Don't feel bad. He can get by with artificial legs later on. The thing is he needs to learn a skill. Listen, Old Li's daughter ..."

"Oh, my name is Spring Flower," she sulked.

"Listen, does your brother have any interests, Spring Flower? If he learns a skill, he won't have to rely on others in the future."

"We could hardly keep our body and soul together. How could we afford any interests? He does like to play with the transistor radio I guess. It was given to my father as an award. One day he pulled it apart, which threw my father into a fit. Later on he was able to put the pieces of junk together and the thing made sounds."

"Good. That seems to be an option. Tell him to keep working hard at it."

Dawei was neither a philanthropist nor a religious man. But he was generous enough to donate all his savings, the loss

of which resulted in the cancellation of
the marriage deal and the matchmaker's
furious ranting. He was downhearted.
The common folks in China lived in
dire poverty, which had become the big
concern of the era. In the countryside,
the peasants, urged to wipe out the last
vestige of capitalism, wound up killing
all the chickens. The five hundred and
fifty yuan was not a hefty amount and
wouldn't go a long way. But it helped to
save a life, the life of a sixteen-year-old.
It filled him with relief and comfort to
see the happy smile on the face of Big
Old Li's daughter whose name he couldn't
manage to remember. He simply didn't
have the heart to turn a blind eye to a
dying man without lifting a hand.

He was still single and in his thirties.
He felt lonely, especially on holidays
when the youngsters in his work shed

had headed home, leaving him alone. His thoughts went drifting back to the light with a yellow halo behind the window. In the deserted work shed, the unshaded bulb shone blinding beams of light at him and added to his loneliness, so unbearable that he would rush out of the work shed to a nearby noodle shop, where he drank himself under the table and spent the night in welcome delirium. Sympathetic folks invited him to their homes for holiday celebrations, but he declined for fear of getting drunk and saying something that could get him into political trouble. Most importantly, he didn't want to be an intruder upon the privacy of others.

To the best of his memory, on one Chinese New Year's Eve, he was eating alone, as often happened, at the almost empty noodle shop, bidding farewell to another year in a melancholy mood.

From outside came the intermittent sounds of firecrackers. Even in this remote mining area the celebrations went on. Temporarily oblivious to the harshness of real life, people were full of joy and jubilation. On the doors of the adobe houses brand new red couplets were posted, adding to the festive atmosphere, though the messages on the couplets remained the same year after year. On an occasion like this he felt keenly the need of a wife, a family.

When he left the restaurant, he found his work shed illuminated by the soft rays of a flashlight, and a wave of warmth swept over him in the freezing wintry night. Who could it be?

"Are you there, Brother Dawei?" asked a girl in a timid but distinctly cheerful voice. It was Big Old Li's daughter.

"Hi, what's up?" What was her name, Cinnamon Flower, Fragrant Flower, or Spring Flower? Hang it, he could never get it right.

"My name is Spring Flower," she reminded him sullenly. He found her face red in the freezing weather.

"Yes, Spring Flower." He was apologetic and swore never to forget her name again. "Why are you standing there in the cold? Who are you waiting for at this time of night?"

"For you." She gave him an imploring look that set his heart astir.

"For me?" he replied in disbelief and perplexity, touching his face unshaven for days. "Is there anything the matter?"

"We're going to have *jiaozi* tonight. My mother would like you to come over for the New Year dinner."

"But I've had dinner already. Thank

you anyway," he was foolish enough to blurt out rashly, trying to conceal his vulnerable feelings. He was good at concealing his inner emotions. A lonely bachelor's life and constantly traveling alone had left him accustomed to keeping himself to himself.

"OK," the girl turned around with a grunt. The snow squeaked as she stepped on it. The night sky on the eve of Chinese New Year was especially clear and transparent. All of a sudden he felt pity for the girl whose face turned red in the biting wind, and regret over his tactless reply.

"Wait a minute, Spring Flower." He hurried to catch up with her but skidded on the snow-covered road. If it hadn't been for Spring Flower grabbing him just in time, he would have fallen flat on his face. Spring Flower got a good kick out of it and laughed. In the distance were sounds of firecracker that heightened the holiday atmosphere.

"Look." Spring Flower shifted her eyesight to the window of the brightly-lit adobe house. The soft light streamed out of the window and covered the trodden snow with a layer of golden yellow. "They can't wait to start, I guess. Do you see the paper flowers pasted on the window? They were cut by my brother. He's got a defter hand than a girl."

The light blinking through the window reminded him of his mother's love for him, which was so distant. It felt wonderful to see a light symbolic of concern and affection. Behind the brightly lit window lay a life of peace and joy, a family content.

"Mom, here is Brother Dawei," Spring Flower cried before she set foot inside the house.

Her mother came out, her hands smeared with flour. Looking at him kindly, she said, "Welcome. We have nothing fancy for dinner, it's just a fun to get together ..." She wasn't even fifty yet, but she was covered with wrinkles and her hair was white. Her eyes, however, shone with pleasure and happiness.

"Old Liu, the leader of the mine, stopped by with pork and flour and wished us a happy holiday. In the old days, a worker's life was worth no more than a dog's life. Old Liu looked sad, as if he were responsible for my husband's death. I told him the mine was a big place and accidents happen, and he was not to be blamed." After saying this she started sobbing.

"Mom!" Spring Flower gave her a reproachful look. "We have a guest and we're celebrating Chinese New Year."

She wiped away the tears and went back to the kitchen to get busy again. On the small wide *kang* table Dawei found an extra pair of chopsticks and a bowl, a tribute to Big Old Li.

"Where's your brother?" he said suddenly, noticing the absence of the boy who had narrowly escaped death.

"He went to ask his friend Erlengzi for some firecrackers. New Year celebrations aren't complete without them, you know."

"Gee! It's pitch dark outside and the road is slippery. And he gets around on crutches. Are you sure he'll be okay?" He was really concerned about the boy.

"Don't worry," Spring Flower replied, not looking up from the *jiaozi* wraps flying from under her rolling pin. "If he's going to have any kind of life, he needs to do things for himself. Nobody is going to care for him forever. He's lost his leg, but not his manhood."

She was right. Her brother couldn't spend the rest of his life as an object of pity, although there was no denying he would have a tougher time than the average person. The last thing he needed was pity. It came to Dawei as a surprise that Spring Flower was capable of such a wise remark. Her name sounded so feminine. As Big Old Li's daughter, she was no different from any other girl in the Gobi Desert, sincere, simple-minded, and hardworking. It was incredible that she could possess so much common sense and a keen insight!

He couldn't help stealing a glance at her. *Jiaozi* wraps continued to be rolled out by her rough but dexterous hands, as big as a man's. She remained so composed and focused. He suddenly noticed that her hair, which used to be thin, dry and yellowish, had turned thick and dark and that her skinny body had grown full and sensual. She was tall and strong, unlike her father. The buxom body beneath her old jacket exuded a sweet alluring fragrance specific to the girl. She enjoyed all the physical features endowed by Providence on a girl. And they burst forth with unstoppable force in much the same way as the desert jujube trees destined to bloom in spring no matter how barren the sandy earth was. The little yellow flowers, though lacking the elegance and beauty of roses and carnations, made the drab and dull desert land appealing with their sweet scent, which spread far and wide.

She noticed his stare. Puzzled, she looked at him and then at herself. Suddenly her whole face turned red. So did his. It was an incredible moment. After all these years in the Gobi Desert, he was capable of getting rowdy or telling a dirty joke with little shame, but he was astonished to find himself still capable of blushing.

"Here I come with firecrackers."

The door was pushed open with a loud bang and in stepped the high-spirited brother. His muscular arms and bright eyes immediately impressed Dawei, who lost sight of the limp pant leg below the boy's knee. "Look at this, a whole string of firecrackers!" He proudly displayed them and then ducked into the inner room.

"I meant to remind him to say thank you to you. But I didn't want to bring the whole thing up again, especially my part," whispered the mother apologetically to Dawei. "We were so shaken up and helpless that day that we almost gave up. Times have changed. Old Liu promised to arrange a job for him, but not now as the country is in trouble. I appreciate his concern anyway." She stopped when she saw the boy pop up beaming from behind the door curtain, with the firecrackers dangling from a twig in his hand.

"Come over here. How come there is a tear in your jacket?" Spring Flower beckoned her brother.

"I fell on the way and it was ripped by the twig," said the excited boy, brushing aside the incident as casually as a hare slipping out of his hands.

"Be careful next time," she scolded him, deftly sewing up the tear in the shoulder of his jacket and then bending down to cut the thread with her teeth. As her face was framed by the thick dark falling hair, he caught a look of sympathy flashing in her eyes.

"Enjoy!" Spring Flower's mother left a full plate of steaming *jiaozi* on the wide *kang* table and her brother unexpectedly produced a bottle of rice wine out of his jacket pocket.

"The bottle almost got broken when I fell. That was a near thing. Mom, don't look at me like that. Today is a special day and I need a drink. Dad always drank at this time of the year, didn't he?" He displayed the bottle of liquor to his mother mischievously and then filled the small cup in front of him. "Let's make a toast to Brother Dawei."

Here was a typical youngster bubbling with youth, self-confidence, and vibrancy. Whatever trauma he had been through was sure to heal with the lapse of time.

"Cheers. To a ..." the boy got stuck, looking around for help. What he wanted to say wasn't easy to sum up in just a few words.

"To a better life in the coming year," Dawei interrupted, coming to his rescue. At the threshold of the new year, he was overwhelmed with a wonderful feeling. Under the soft light of the bulb hanging low from the beam, he had never before found himself in such an optimistic mood. His heart was warm, not with the alcohol he had consumed, but with a recovered sense of family serenity and cohesiveness.

Spring Flower's mother served him with a large bowlful of *jiaozi*.

"How pleased my husband would be to see you with us at New Year! He told me he invited you over several times, but you wouldn't come. And he didn't insist, partially because our daughter was still young and unmarried and we feared the gossip."

"Mom ..." Spring Flower lightly struck the edge of her bowl, looking reproachfully at her, then glancing apologetically at Dawei. He felt awkward to witness the embarrassing scene between mother and daughter.

"Go and set off the firecrackers," Dawei urged Spring Flower's brother.

Shoving aside the bowl and chopsticks, he grabbed the firecrackers and got off the *kang*, but in his hurry he smashed a wine cup.

"Peace, peace. May the New Year bring peace!" The superstitious mother muttered a homophone for "piece" over and over, trying to avert bad luck.

"Don't blame him, Mom," Spring Flower intervened. "Can't you see he's over the moon today? The poor kid almost missed the New Year."

Outside the door, firecrackers exploded with a deafening roar. Spring Flower's brother hopped around having enormous fun. The roar broke through the silence of the vast desert, which stretched as far as the eye could see under a cloudless sky. Dawei hadn't seen such a clear and bright sky for many years.

"Thank you for everything," Spring Flower whispered almost inaudibly. "You're very, very kind."

Dawei turned to look at her, baffled and tongue-tied. Years later, he blamed himself for his timidity and clumsiness. He should have said something, instead of standing there like a fool. Spring Flower's lips quivered, and with a disappointed look she turned around to step back inside. He wanted to give her a few words of comfort, but the words never left his mouth.

"So you were too shy to say something?" Xiao'an faced Dawei with a sly look.

"Not at all." He gazed at his two rough hands. "I didn't want to take advantage of their misfortune. My donation could have been misconstrued as trading money for marriage. Every one in that family has a pure heart and I didn't want to do anything to tarnish or blemish that. Only tenacious folks can make it in the Gobi. The hard life there hasn't knocked the spirit out of them; they remain as pure, warm, and sincere as ever. There in the desert, men of the world are frowned upon and down-to-earth, easy-going folks are well thought of. Girls need to be unpretentious and modest to be liked. Just think, my folks in Shanghai are locked in ferocious fights, each after their own selfish ends. Family sentiments don't exist for them and my stepmother is cracking up because of her bickering children. Only genuine friendship forged in the most adverse circumstances can stand the test of time."

"I have a question that remains unanswered and I'm determined to get to the bottom of it," Xiao'an said thoughtfully, while biting her fingernail. "Is it true that material life is in reverse proportion to moral standards; I mean, the more abundant material life is, the lower the moral standards; or conversely the more depraved the former, the higher the latter? If it's true, why do we work so hard to improve our living standards?"

What a question! He had never really thought about it. But he was positive, based on his harsh experience in the Gobi Desert, that an individual who lived isolated in comfort and luxury too long would end up being arrogant and self-centered, and be reduced to not much more than a zombie!

"We may both have belonged to that category once, but it's been done away with in my case and will soon be in your case. We shouldn't get sucked in by a lifestyle that is attractive but depraved. With a lifestyle like that, there's no chance of being a fresh flower, just a gorgeous replica devoid of life. How tragic it is to be an imitation flower!"

Xiao'an listened quietly, watching him tenderly, and holding his hand in her own while the cool night breeze blew in from the sea. She said, "I envy you because I'm not living a true life and I have no knowledge or experience of the real world."

That was the tragedy of her life. He, on the other hand, had experienced the best as well as the worst life had to offer, from the bunkers in the Gobi Desert to the six-story residential buildings that had mushroomed in the newly developed mining town.

"You're tormented by love, aren't you? The greater the torment, the mellower and sweeter love is," he teased her.

"It can hardly be called torment. I'm going to write him a letter every day, telling him I love him with my heart and soul. I won't stop until I get a reply from him and I'll be persistent like your Chrysanthemum, excuse me, your Spring Flower. Speaking of her, how come you two ended up tying the knot?" She had composed herself again, knowing what strategy to adopt with her boyfriend.

"No comment."

"Is it a secret?"

"Yes and no. There are certain things deep in your heart you aren't supposed to share with others."

"I see." She was in a good mood, humming a tune. "It's nine o'clock and still early. Why don't we go and dance?"

"Dance?"

"Yes. When you were young, you weren't smart enough. But when you became smart, you were unlucky enough to be thrown into the Cultural Revolution. Now that the storm is over we can play as hard as we want for as long as we want."

The little girl seemed to be good at offering advice to others, but when she hit trouble herself she was helpless and weepy. Dawei thought himself wise to have lent her a hand when she needed it most.

The ball room was brightly lit. The

first piece of music stopped, followed by laughter and murmuring before the next piece struck up with the oboe and French horn initiating the enchanting prelude. To a smooth and soothing accompaniment, the violin solo played a familiar poetic tune as if pouring out a steam of inner emotions. It was a song overflowing with love and tenderness, one promising a future of hope and happiness, and one he had missed for twenty years. The song was *When a Baby Is Born*.

As the gentle melody lifted him to a lofty world, he had been awakened from a deep slumber by the tune that symbolized the promise of his youth but, sadly, brought his first love to an abrupt dead end. He wasn't sure if his feet were stepping in time with the music; but he was sure he was floating on the glorious string of notes.

The turnover of the welders in the mining area was pretty high. Shortly after the Chinese New Year, he was transferred to another mining district, which was a newly developed district short of skilled welders.

"Are you transferring, Brother Dawei?" Spring Flower met him at the work site. She was no longer involved in her tea chores, but in making adobe bricks. She was still off the official payroll.

"Wherever I go, I work for the mine," he said, ready to cut the conversation short and walk away, but she approached and met his eyes with a strange look of despondency.

"Will you stop by and see us often?" she asked anxiously.

"Sure, my new job isn't far from here," he said, reassuring himself more than her.

Finally, unable to bear the tension, she walked back to her job.

"Forgive me, Spring Flower," Dawei murmured in his heart. She was a model of beauty and perfection. He wouldn't accept her love before he could make a commitment to loving her whole-heartedly and unreservedly. She was too good to be spoiled. She wasn't the same type as the accountant he had meant to marry.

True love can be substantiated by a period of separation. Once he had lost sight of the full, well-developed body of Spring Flower, he felt like a lost soul and realized he was completely in love with her. He kept telling himself night and day that he had to see her again. He was astonished that he was experiencing the emotions of his first love for a second time, and that he felt so mesmerized, uncertain, and yet elated by it. He was in a complex emotional state, swinging from euphoria to depression.

"Can I come and see you this Saturday?" he said when he finally called her, but it was silent on the other end. "You got it, Spring Flower? I'm coming," he said fretfully.

He heard quiet sobs on the line.

There were howling gusts of wind that day, as was often the case in the Gobi. His mouth, nostrils, and ears were assaulted by the sand swirling in the violent wind. He borrowed a bike and, like a man in love for the first time, frantically pedaled thinking only of their future together. Blinded by the sand, he got lost, but eventually found his way to where she lived. Night had fallen and it was completely dark. But in the distance a light was flickering behind a window. Spring Flower was waiting for him. What a wonderful feeling to have someone who was looking forward to his arrival! A lonely chapter in his life was about to end.

"I'm plain and uneducated. I'm no good for you," Spring Flower protested feebly. "You're from Shanghai and I'm a country girl."

"Cut it out," he said. He smothered her with a long kiss. The issue of good or no good didn't exist in their relationship, only the desperate need for each other.

The early days of their marriage made him giddy with happiness. In truth he had found a collaborator in his life, someone to share the burdens and make his life more rewarding. She was more a partner than a wife.

The heavy demands of her life meant that she couldn't afford to think of herself as a woman. She wore her husband's old work jacket and her thinning hair had rarely been near a beautician's comb or hairdryer. Only recently was she dragged by her friends to a newly opened beauty salon, fitted out with elaborate perming equipment, where she only had a blow dry. She wouldn't have a perm for anything. "Paying two yuan and five jiao for a hellish time under a hood? You have to be kidding!" Because she had never worn a bra, which was a novelty she had only recently spotted in a department store with wonder and shock, her breasts sagged down her flat chest, leaving no curves in profile. As far as her husband was concerned, she was a woman, a genuinely kind woman being nurtured by his tender love, a woman who reciprocated with a desire to look attractive to her husband.

When their sheep pen was wrecked by a windstorm and they were frantically saving the few trapped young lambs, their only property, a chunk of adobe wall fell and landed on Dawei's left leg, inflicting such excruciating pain that he fell down, on the verge of passing out. While pulling a lamb with all her strength, his wife yelled at him, "Can't you give me a hand? You're a man. Get a grip on yourself and pull, will you?" He gritted his teeth and struggled to get up despite the piercing pain. For an instant, he felt his wife was being too hard on him. When the wind had subsided, his disabled brother-in-law showed up with a transistor radio he had just repaired, which he wanted to show off to his sister. Seeing the boy's triumphant smile, he realized that she was right to set the bar high for him, rather than spoil him. She pinned as much hope on her brother, who had conquered his disability, as on her own husband, who she expected to fulfill his share of duties with absolute courage. She had complete trust in him and her voice seemed to constantly ring in his ears, "I've given you my whole life and you've given me yours." Spring Flower would have been an outstanding professional if she had received a college education. He had no doubt about that.

But she also had her moments of weakness, self-confident as she was. The night before he left to attend school following the receipt of the letter of admission to college, she burst into tears, helpless and devastated. Underneath her pillow, he found a small oval mirror. He used to think his wife never cared how she looked. He had been wrong, knowing nothing about when or where she had secretly purchased the "luxury" item.

Now that he understood, he started to comfort and console her and, like all women, once she was showered with tenderness and affection, she reacted with an even more unabashed display of her feelings by indulging in convulsions of sobbing on his chest, with complete abandon.

"You're part of me. To leave you would be as good as cutting off my limbs. Do you think I'm out of my mind?" he assured his wife, followed by unrestrained kisses on her cheeks and eyelids. That night, they relived their wedding night.

The town was thriving, crammed with department stores well stocked with all kinds of consumer goods for women, such as pearl cream, vanishing cream, hair tonic, and even lacey bras; everything under the sun. It was a shame that she was past the prime of youth. But she wasn't the jealous type. Whenever they came across a well-dressed girl in high heels as they strolled through the new business area of the town, she would make flattering comments, "How cool our girls are! They are not bad looking at all, compared with Shanghai girls. Look at that girl's shapely body and her tiny waist. She walks along light as a feather. Cool! I wish I had a daughter so I could dress her up."

"But we'll have a daughter-in-law instead, and you could dress her up any way you like. But first of all we should do something to make you pretty."

"So you think I'm an old hag?" She looked at him with a teasing smile.

"Spring Flower, you've had a tough time all these years and you don't even have a decent jacket."

"That's all right. Our future daughter-in-law will make up for it. I'll get her as many beautiful clothes as I can. Look at the T-shirt with a rainbow on it. It's so colorful and fantastic! Is it made in Shanghai? I'll definitely get this one for her. The coat over there is nice, too, and it'll look good on someone with a shapely body like our future daughter-in-law. I'm sure she'll look sharp with the coat on. I promise to get her tons of clothes."

That day, despite Spring Flower's objections, he bought her two gifts: a bottle of perfume and a bottle of cream, both made in Shanghai and beautifully packaged. The glass bottles with gleaming golden lids on top were a deep blue color and exquisitely made. They were more like works of art than cosmetic items. At first, she complained about wasting five yuan. But she grew very fond of them when she got home. When she tidied up the room every day, she would polish the two attractive bottles with a piece of cloth. She treasured them too much to open them. Maybe she wanted to keep them for their future daughter-in-law. Women's accessories, especially such elaborately designed and packaged cosmetics as these, have a glamorous appeal. The trivial additions brightened the mood of the house. He was charmed, but slightly sad, to see them displayed on the chest of drawers either side of the oval mirror. He was wondering whether girls, while busy selecting beautiful clothes and cosmetics with covetous and choosy eyes, ever thought of their self-sacrificing mothers and all the other females who had generously given their best.

"What happened, Dawei?" Xiao'an asked

him, seeing tears in his eyes.

"It's been twenty years since I listened to that song," he replied emotionally.

He couldn't believe twenty years had passed without his knowing it, in the course of which the barren stretch of land had been transformed into a new-born town, fresh and delicate. With the birth of a baby, the fear, pain, and anxiety associated with labor disappeared. All that was left in a mother's heart was love and pride. Some time ago, filling out his son's application for elementary school, he solemnly put down Gansu as his birthplace.

Chapter 4

The train rolled on with a lullaby-like rhythm, bringing him closer and closer to his home where his wife was waiting anxiously to see him. He looked up again at the faded traveling bag that contained two pounds of red woolen yarns. Furthermore he entrusted Xiao'an his three-hundred-yuan bonus to purchase some pretty clothes from Shanghai for his wife with the intention of buying back some of her youth if he could.

"How come your map has a little dot

marking a new town and mine doesn't?"

"Yours is the 1973 edition. It's totally outdated. As far as I know, the designation of that place as a new town was approved by the State Council only last year."

Two college students, who were used to late nights, were studying their atlas.

"But it's a very small town. Is it worth the State Council's trouble?"

"Large or small, a town is a town, isn't it?"

Dawei was on the point of telling them that so much sweat had been shed and so many pleasures in life sacrificed in order for the little dot to appear on the map. His wife, Spring Flower, who had contributed her share to the birth of the new town, was still without a legal urban resident status or a regular job. Complaining was foreign to them. The town was all but a delicate new-born baby with a fragile skeleton unable to sustain a heavy weight. Tall residential buildings had sprung up everywhere, but they still huddled in their adobe house. They could afford to wait as time was on their side. The numerous scaffolds here and there were an affirmation that adobe houses would soon be history. My dear baby, grow big and strong as soon as you can.

It was late at night and the loudspeaker said good night to the passengers. Normally, at this time, his son would look up at him. "Are you reading tonight, Dad?" If he didn't, the kid would sneak under his quilt and bug him for stories about Shanghai. He had made up his mind to take the whole family on a trip to the city at Spring Festival this year. Xiao'an had promised to go and meet them at the railway station. What a change that would be! Now there was someone in his native town waiting for his return. As Shanghai was plunged into a blaze of lights at nightfall, one light was intended for him. His brother-in-law, who had returned with his mother to their home village where he worked as a well-liked TV repairman with a good income, had recently written to tell him that he had saved enough money to get himself a pair of artificial limbs in Shanghai. "I want to stand up and walk without crutches," he said. He didn't have the education to realize that they wouldn't function properly until he had gone through a period of training and adjustment. It was a good investment, he thought. A factory situated on Jiaozhou Road in Shanghai specialized in making equipment to help the disabled. But he needed to contact Xiao'an and talk it over with her first. It was gratifying to know someone back there in his place of birth that cared him.

Xiao'an, who was as pure and innocent as a child, was sure to grow into a mature and strong woman of the world. She was totally different from Xiaomei in the sense that her career had renewed her and that rejuvenating process would continue with her boyfriend. A life of fulfillment awaited her.

"Ouch, the baby is kicking again," whispered a voice in the lower berth. "It gives me no peace at night." It was Mr. T-shirt's wife. Eager to share her joy with her husband, and despite the surroundings, she was making an excited fuss.

Hearing his wife's voice, Mr. T-shirt jumped out of bed and their whispers and murmurs were lost in the rattle of the train.

Unexpectedly, Dawei lost his hostility towards Mr. T-shirt. The birth of a new life would bring hope and expectation, a yearning and a sense of beauty. The peaceful, enchanting melody of *When a Baby Is Born* played in his heart. He hated the way people like Mr. T-shirt believed in waiting complacently for everything to come to them, usually at the expense of others, rather than the concept of give-and-take. However, he was ready to make an exception for Mr. T-shirt, who just might see sense and change his values after becoming a father.

With an impassioned heart, he sincerely wished the baby, and all the others ready to leap into this world, a life of complete joy and happiness that would transcend his own.

Stories by Contemporary Writers from Shanghai